When nine-year-old Ulla Lundgren arrived in the United States everything in the new country was strange to her. At home, in Sweden, Ulla had known what was expected of her—and she had friends and her grandmother to visit. But here everything was new and unfamiliar. And it didn't help when her whole family: Mamma, Pappa, Sven, Pelle, and even Aunt Elsa seemed at home and busy in their new country.

Ulla felt herself getting prickly all over—and sulky and unhappy. She had no friend to talk to, she did not understand the language, she could not understand her schoolwork, and she was sure all the other girls were laughing at her and her clothes.

It didn't happen right away, but slowly Ulla learned to reach out—and then her world expanded!

A Feast of Light

⊹ჰⴹ⊹

A Feast of Light

by Gunilla Norris

Illustrated by Nancy Grossman

Alfred A. Knopf: New York

This is a Borzoi Book published by Alfred A. Knopf, Inc.

Library of Congress Catalog Card Number: 67-15804

To Mappa with love

Contents

A Feast of Light

One

They Arrive

The big horn of the ocean liner blasted into the late morning air. The sound of it went right into Ulla's ears and seemed to explode there. Or perhaps it was excitement that was going off like firecrackers inside her head—and in her stomach.

There she was, Ulla Lundgren, ten years old, standing on the deck of an ocean liner, looking at New York City for the very first time. And beside her was little Pelle, his eyes as big as truck wheels. Sven, too, was there looking grown up with brown hair slicked down. It must be nice to be thirteen, Ulla thought, and envied him. There, next to them all, was plump Aunt Elsa with her usual frown. Probably she was counting suitcases in her mind and going through their passports for the hundred and ninth time. She had a way of being busy and of darting in every direction to accomplish nothing at all. Ulla thought it must be because Aunt Elsa's clothes were too tight and they made her uncomfortable.

Ulla jumped at the second blast. It was a long majestic roar. She found herself too excited to stand still. She wanted to wave her arms and give a big yell.

"Do stay still," Aunt Elsa said in Swedish, pacing up and down behind them. "We'll be there all too soon."

"Just think!" cried Ulla. "We'll see Mamma and Pappa in just one hour. I can't bear the waiting."

"Mamma?" asked Pelle.

"Yes, your Mamma." Ulla squeezed him. "You can't have forgotten her already, silly goose, even if you are only three. She and Pappa have been away only six months, after all."

Oh, but what a long time that had been and how she had cried when they left. Sven had told her to be sensible.

Their parents were only going to America for Pappa's new work. It would take time to find a home and to get everything ready.

Sven himself, of course, was very sensible and didn't show that he missed them very much. Perhaps in his bed at night he had missed them. Perhaps he even cried. But otherwise he was his old, calm self. As for herself, Ulla showed everyone how she felt. Grandmother called her a weather vane because at the slightest provocation tears would come or those nonstop giggles or mean sparks of anger. It was a nuisance. At times even Ulla became completely mixed up in the turnings of her feelings.

And now the excitement was gnawing at her like a persistent mouse. She turned to Sven to share it, but he was busy looking at the tugboats maneuvering in the great Hudson River. His eyes squinted with concentration.

She squatted down beside Pelle who, with mouth open, was absorbing the whole scene: the wisps of smoke from the liner's two smokestacks, the sharp cry of gulls in the late September air, the creaking of the decks and the gentle swaying of the lifeboats on their hooks. Pelle sucked in a little drool and sighed with pleasure.

Ulla turned to Aunt Elsa, but she had collapsed into a deck chair, her face flushed and her plump hands fluttering to her forehead like doves to a perch.

Ulla had no one to talk to and the excitement kept growing inside of her. She made herself lean up against the deck's railing. The wind pushed through her light brown hair and it soothed her a little. The wind made her think of Grandmother's hands stroking her hair, of sitting next to Grandmother at home in Sweden. How they would sit on the wooden settee in the hall and talk! Grandmother was the only person in the world who could understand her perfectly well. Grandmother was not put out by all the different feelings that kept cropping up in her like strange mushrooms in a field.

Seeing Mamma and Pappa would be wonderful. Coming to America was too exciting to endure. But she would always feel that little hollow space inside her that had first come when she said good-by to Grandmother. As long as Ulla could remember Grandmother had lived just down the street. Ulla shut her eyes and tried to picture the familiar things. She could smell the apples in the bowl on the table in the living room; the soft smell of dust in the reading corner where the dog-eared books were heaped. She could feel the smooth piano bench under her legs—cool and slippery—where she and Grandmother sat down to sing. It had been a wonderful

six months even with Mamma and Pappa away. Ulla wished one could wrap memories in small packages to keep them the same, always.

She opened her eyes. Below, the gray water leaped up against the ocean liner. The small tugs labored up the harbor, the liner a huge, helpless weight behind them. Buildings rose before her, taller than she imagined possible. It was lovely and frightening. She took Pelle's hand and felt his soft, warm palm. He stood there flat-footed and secure as if to say—America will be a nice place for a small Swedish boy like me.

And just then, ahead of them on a pier jutting out into the river, she saw a small figure waving a pinpoint of a hat.

"That's Pappa," she said. "Pelle, Sven, Aunt Elsa, I see Pappa! I know it is!" She called at the top of her lungs and Aunt Elsa turned crimson with embarrassment for her. But Ulla didn't care. In a short while the tugs maneuvered the liner alongside the pier and the boat was docking. Looking over the deck railing, she spotted Mamma eagerly looking for her children. Pappa was giving his small mustache reassuring strokes from time to time as though that would hold his excitement down. To Ulla it was unbearable to have to wait for the others. Aunt Elsa seemed to have taken no notice of their arrival in the persistent arranging of her pocketbook. First came the passports in a neat row, then the hair combs, the hat pins, the small bottle of lavender, a Swedish paper flag wrapped neatly in pink tissue paper and lastly her enameled pillbox filled with tiny hard candies and sugar-coated chocolate buttons. These items were arranged and rearranged until she was satisfied. America could wait as far as Aunt Elsa was concerned, and everyone on the dock could wait as well.

At last they were gathered together. Sven took command of their three small suitcases and led the way to the gangplank. He always had presence of mind and it made Ulla a little angry. Never did Sven seem ruffled. Never was he messy. Grandmother said it was exceedingly strange for a boy of thirteen to be like that, but she reassured Ulla that Sven must have his moments, too.

Now Ulla became aware of herself. How messy she looked. She had not pulled her socks up, and her hair hung in bunches. She really should have taken more care, but now they were moving at last down the gangplank, past the passport booth and finally into the waiting crowd.

Mamma found them in a moment. "Welcome, darlings," she said in Swedish and dispatched a ready hug to each of them. Pappa's peppercorn eyes blinked happily. Pelle, not satisfied with only one hug, stretched his fat arms to his mother. She picked him up and he settled his head near her neck with a sigh of recognition. Now they waited for Aunt Elsa who had been caught among the milling people.

"There she is," said Sven. "I'll fetch her."

In a moment he was back and Mamma kissed her sister warmly.

"Thank heavens for Sven," said Pappa.

Ulla could not look at her parents. She was sure they would never be as proud of her as they were of Sven. But Pappa didn't give her a chance to dwell on that depressing thought. He gave his mustache a small twist and said, "Let's be going. We want to go home, now, don't we?"

Of course, that is what they wanted more than anything else after eight days on the boat. But now Ulla began to wonder what home in America would be like.

Two

About the House

&8

Home as it turned out, was a large house in Westchester
County that Pappa had bought very cheaply, and natu-
rally it had a few things wrong with it. The roof leaked
slightly and the plumbing gurgled. Some of the doors
would not close properly, and some of the plaster had
peeled off in decorative patches. Other than that, the
house was splendid and everyone said so, except Aunt
Elsa, who thought it was much too large. On that very

first morning she had stamped up and down the three flights of stairs muttering that housekeeping would be beyond her.

"How do you decide where to begin?" she asked.

But Mamma reassured her, saying, "Never mind, dear." Aunt Elsa had lived with them so long that no one could imagine home without her. She had come to help Mamma when Sven and Ulla were little and then she had just stayed. Pappa said she stayed because it was too hard for her to make up her mind to do anything else. And, of course, she still helped in a pinch, but mostly she was just there.

Pappa, on the other hand, had made up his mind from the start just where to begin. On that first morning he took Ulla out in the garden.

"I want you to see something," he said with a sheepish grin.

"Where? What?" said Ulla, not knowing where to look as she stumbled through garden weeds that came up to her waist.

"Here," said Pappa and laughed. "Don't you see?"

And when Ulla came up to where Pappa was standing, she saw. In the middle of all the weeds were three flower

beds with the weeds all pulled and the earth turned as neatly as could be.

"I've been doing my favorite kind of housekeeping," said Pappa. "In that earth I'll put all kinds of flowers and bulbs and by spring we'll have a garden to look at. But only the family will know just yet. It's kind of a secret until spring."

Ulla smiled. "No one can see from the street, can they?"

"No," said Pappa. "Besides, no one bothers to look. Everyone in this neighborhood calls this place an eyesore."

"Aye soar?" said Ulla wonderingly, rolling the funny English word on her tongue. "What is that?"

"Well, Ulla," said Pappa, "I don't think we have a Swedish word just like it, but it means that the house and the yard are ugly to look at."

"But, Pappa!" said Ulla indignantly. "It's beautiful, better than the palace of Drottningholm!"

"There you are," said Pappa with a grin. "You have to have eyes to see what can be done. Look around."

Ulla did. From where she stood she saw neatly trimmed yards and well-groomed houses.

"We don't look as neat as that," said Pappa. "But you

wait. In a short time we'll have this garden blooming and the house as fresh as new laundry."

Ulla looked at her father and nodded. Of course, they would. Ulla knew Pappa was good at fixing things, and gardening he loved best of all.

"You had better run along now," said Pappa. "I have to figure out what kind of plants and bulbs will grow best in America. There's a lot of work to do."

As Ulla walked back to the house she thought about Pappa's secret and she wondered about the eyesore word. How could a house be an eyesore when it had a bedroom for Mamma and Pappa; separate bedrooms for Pelle, Ulla, and Sven; a whole third floor for Aunt Elsa; a big cobwebby attic for Mamma to paint pictures in; a big musty cellar for Sven's model building; a kitchen; a dining room; a living room with a fireplace for the whole family; and last, a mud room? No. The more she thought about the house the more she was convinced that she would never live in a grander one. Why, earlier that morning she had discovered that she could stand in her room and yell at the top of her voice and the sound would carry as far as the attic and down to the boiler! That deserved top rating. She had to write Grandmother all about everything. She had to do it right away.

Ulla ran inside and dashed up the stairs to her room. She sat down by her desk and began at once.

Dear Mormor,

We live in a house far better than the palace of Drottningholm. I have a room all to myself. It has blue wallpaper. And I have a bed with just the right hollow in the middle. My desk has a wobbly front leg and my bureau is bright yellow. Sven and Pelle have their own rooms, too.

Guess what? When I shout everyone can hear from top to bottom. It is all lovely. Not aye-soar at all. Tell my friends. I love you.

From,

Ulla

Ulla looked at her letter with satisfaction, and then she looked at her room. It was her first very own room and it was lovely.

In the few days that followed, Pelle broke off most of the loose plaster that he could reach. He went around with the sweet smile that satisfaction brings.

Sven cleared out the cellar and showed up at meals smelling of damp concrete, mold, and rust.

During the afternoons, Aunt Elsa was not to be seen at

all. She kept to the third floor and said she was recuperating from the past week's hard work of traveling. By the sound of it, however, there was a great deal of bustling, tapping, sliding, and stamping. Mamma said that Aunt Elsa was having a wonderful time fretting about where she would *not* put the furniture.

Pappa, of course, had walked to the commuting train and was in the great city of New York selling Swedish office machines.

The old house rocked with new sounds during those first days. Sounds that bulged through the curtains and leaped through the house cracks. Sounds that traveled through the weedy garden and out into the street. They were busy sounds, bustling, happy sounds. Up and down went the Swedish words in a kind of singsong. But Ulla, who was dashing about in the middle of all the excitement, somehow began to feel uneasy. Her uneasiness grew and she went to her room at last and curled up in the hollow of the bed. She tried to think why she suddenly felt afraid. All those nice sounds in the old house began to fade. Faintly, Ulla could hear Pelle building with his blocks and from down below she could hear the muffled rattling of Mamma's pots. Everything grew still. Why was everything so quiet? Why didn't everybody keep talking and bustling?

Then suddenly she heard something—not from their house but from far away. It was the sound of a rake against a sidewalk. It was the sound of a car starting. It was the broad, deep sound of English. Someone was calling. The sound of the world beyond the window was coming in and Ulla paid attention. Those sounds had been trying to get in all the time and no one had listened. Ulla went down the stairs slowly and walked to the front door. For a while she hesitated with her hand on the doorknob. And then, finally, she opened the door and looked out.

Ulla saw a girl standing on the sidewalk with a jump rope in her hand. The girl had seen the door open. She noticed Ulla standing there and she started up the driveway.

"I didn't know there was a girl here," said the girl. "When did you come?"

Ulla shook her head. The words she heard were flat and broad. They made no sense. The girl watched Ulla with curiosity.

"Don't you talk?" she asked and pointed to Ulla's mouth with a long finger.

Ulla felt confused. The words seemed harsh. Was the girl making fun of her?

"Jag talar Svenska," said Ulla, and felt her face flush. Why did the girl point like that? No one was going to point at her. This was her home. Quickly she slammed the door and ran upstairs.

Three

Pappa Gives a Lesson

Ulla told no one what had happened. A week went by. Then one evening Pappa announced that Ulla and Sven were to begin school the next day.

"Mamma and I thought you should have a week," he said, "to get used to our new home and to get all settled. Tomorrow it is time to begin school."

Ulla had known all along that this was coming, but she had put it out of her mind. Sven shifted in his chair and took it all calmly. But he, after all, had been old enough to study English in his Swedish school. Ulla was only in the fourth grade and she would not have had English until the fifth grade in her old school. Pelle, the lucky boy, was not even in school at all and he could stay at home with his blocks. Ulla looked at Pappa as if to say, "Do I have to?" And Pappa's peppery eyes snapped right back at her—"Of course you have to!"

Ulla pushed the food around her plate. How could she go to school when she couldn't understand a word of English and when she did not know anyone? She was sure the children would only point at her. "I don't want to go to school," she mumbled under her breath, but everyone heard her.

"That will be quite enough," said Pappa. "You are going to school and that is that." The Swedish words rumbled across the table.

Pelle opened his mouth to cry.

Aunt Elsa blew her nose and said, "Really, Ulla!"

With all of them looking at her, Ulla began to grow stubborn. She set her jaw and fixed her eyes on the cold potatoes on her plate.

"You must go to school," said Pappa. "Children all over the world do and you, Ulla Lundgren, will be no exception. You must continue to learn."

The cold potatoes on Ulla's plate began to look fuzzy the way things do when you have looked at them much too hard.

"If there's anything worse than a stubborn Swedish boy, it's a stubborn Swedish girl," said Aunt Elsa icily, and tapped her nervous fingers on the tablecloth.

Pappa looked a little crossly at Aunt Elsa. "It isn't easy to learn a new language," he said, but Ulla had already jumped up and run from the table, into the hall, up the stairs, and to her room. From downstairs, the creaking springs of Ulla's iron bed could be heard.

"Oh dear," said Aunt Elsa with a sigh. "I'll never understand."

"Never mind," said Mamma, trying to make peace. "It's no use for everyone to get worked up."

Pelle had decided not to cry and went on eating his dinner peacefully. Sven thought about glue, the best glue for the next delicate step in building a model ship.

"I'll go up," said Pappa. Thoughtfully he stroked his mustache as he climbed the stairs.

Ulla could hear someone coming. She put her head under the pillow. She recognized Pappa's footsteps.

"If I must speak to an ostrich, I will," said Pappa and

sat down on the bed. "First of all, we have settled all opposition about going to school. Isn't that so?"

Ulla failed to answer.

"Very well, I never expected an ostrich to come right out and speak to me. However," Pappa twirled his mustache, "I thought you might like to learn some English before you begin school tomorrow."

Ulla listened under the pillow. It was beginning to get very warm for her.

"We will begin with the first lesson. It goes like this, *'My name is Ulla Lundgren.'* " Pappa translated the sentence into Swedish and repeated, " *'My name is Ulla Lundgren.'* "

From under her pillow Ulla slowly shaped the queer, broad words on her tongue. "Maye naym is Ulla Lundgren." But she made no sound.

"Have you got that?" Pappa asked.

There was only a grunt from under the pillow.

"All right then, we are ready for the second lesson. *'I do not understand English.'* That is the most useful sentence on the first day," said Pappa. He told her what it meant. "Just smile prettily and say, *'I do not understand English.'* People will be most happy to help you because once their great-grandparents were in just the same predicament. Once again, repeat with me, '*I do not understand English.*' "

Ulla said the words in her head. Pappa waited for some sign before he went on. Ulla's head felt as if she had a fever of 102 degrees. She wiggled her toes and tried not to breathe so much hot air into the pillow.

"Shall we go on?" asked Pappa. "Well?"

Ulla wiggled her toes in reply.

"Here is the third lesson. '*I wish to learn.*' " He spoke the foreign words slowly. Then he said them in Swedish. "That, dear Ulla, is one of the most important sentences in any language. But, of course, you must also mean it when you say it. You must work hard. Then it will make miracles for you. '*I wish to learn!*' It almost sounds like music."

From under her pillow Ulla whispered, "Aye weesh tou lurn." But to her it didn't sound like music at all.

"That's enough, I believe," said Pappa at last. "I hope you have paid attention. Aren't you terribly warm under there?" he asked as he went to the door.

Ulla held her breath.

"Never mind, my little ostrich. You can come out when I go for my coffee." He closed the door behind him softly.

After a while Ulla brought her rumpled head out in the open and sat up.

"Aye duh nut unnerstan Eenglish," she said and her mouth felt awkward and stiff. "Aye duh nut unnerstan," she repeated, "Aye duh nut . . . Aye duh nut . . . Aye duh nut!" Finally, she made a fearful grimace in the mirror. It made her feel ever so much better. In fact, she even giggled.

Four

School

₊₃₈₊

It was seven-thirty by the clock when Mamma, Sven, and Ulla started out into the chilly October morning. Mamma had her old brown coat on, but she had added the fur piece worn only on special occasions. It consisted of the heads and fur of two little foxes that snapped together like a muffler around her neck. Ulla had on one of her two skirts, long woolly stockings that hitched to her under-shirt and a big green sweater over her blouse. Her hair was braided tightly and tied with large purple ribbons. Mamma was satisfied that the female part of the family looked neat and clean. Sven was always neat anyway, though how he managed it Mamma could never figure out. She had stopped worrying long ago. Sven seemed a normal boy, though an amazingly clean one. Ulla and Pelle made up for him in any case.

It took them one-half hour to walk to school. By then Ulla's hair had produced a dozen stray wisps. Her purple bows wilted on the two stubby braids. Her stockings had big rolls above the knees and her blouse tail hung out under the sweater. Mamma shook her head, tried to remedy the damage and took the children to the principal's office. At home, they had agreed that Sven was to do the talking since he spoke the best English.

"My name is Sven Lundgren. This is my sister, Ulla," said Sven.

"Nice to meet you," said the principal, looking over his glasses.

Ulla said nothing at all while Mamma and Sven went on with the business of enrolling her in school. She stared at all the office machines and the big electric clocks on every wall. Sven would have to go to another school called a Junior High School. She was to be left with the principal, the machines, and the clocks.

When they were all done, Mamma gave Ulla a reassuring pat on her shoulder. "After school, you can walk home on your own," she said in Swedish. "Have a good day, darling."

Sven waved and they were gone. Ulla could feel the butterflies banging against her stomach walls. She looked up at the principal. He smiled at her very gently, but behind the smile was a "No Nonsense" look.

Ulla's classroom was one of those big airy rooms with at least thirty desks, and paper leaves pasted on every window. When she came into the room, Ulla could feel twenty-nine pairs of eyes going over her. She could see twenty-nine smiles on twenty-nine curious faces. It was very awful and she felt a good deal like sticking out her tongue. But she thought better of it. Before he left, the principal spoke to the class, and Ulla understood nothing at all. Then the teacher spoke to the class and Ulla still understood nothing at all. At last she saw the teacher writing her name on the blackboard.

"Youla," the teacher pronounced it and the class repeated, "Youla."

No, no, that wasn't it at all. Ulla shook her head and turned red.

"No Youla," she said. "Ulla."

The class snickered. The teacher was embarrassed and spoke to the class. "Yuhlla," they all tried.

"No, no." Ulla frowned. She shaped her mouth into an o. "U . . . U . . . Ulla," she said and waited.

But now the class thought it was hilarious. They all cried, "Uh, Uh, Uh!"

"Very well for you," thought Ulla disgustedly, along with some other dark Swedish thoughts.

By now the teacher was very much embarrassed, and she also felt quite sorry for Ulla. Quickly she said some more things to the students and the class settled down. The teacher showed Ulla to a desk and school began in earnest.

They did arithmetic for an hour. Ulla looked at the blackboard. What was everyone doing? She guessed at division and was pleased with herself for figuring it out. But divisions weren't set up in the familiar sensible way with a vertical line broken at the middle by a horizontal line going off to the right. Instead, the problems were put in a kind of backward Z. And then came other problems, not drawn on the blackboard at all. Those were the ones the teacher gave out loud and Ulla understood not a word. She had to be content to look about the classroom.

At recess her classmates gathered around her. To their many questions she could only say, "Aye duh nut unnerstan Eenglish."

Finally, she ended up by shaking her head until the bell rang and another hour of school began. This hour was spelling. Never had Ulla seen such queer combinations of letters. Not one word was pronounced as it was spelled. Twenty-nine pencils scribbled busily in the spelling books and hers was the only one lying helplessly on the desk top. It was as if everyone were taking a train ride while she stood alone watching them all go by.

It was the same with reading and social studies, with geography and the new American games in the gymnasium. By three o'clock, Ulla was utterly tired. She had repeated, "Aye duh nut unnerstan Eenglish," more times than she could count. She had pronounced her name so often that she was even tired of it herself. It had been a very hard day. The air buzzed with sounds she could not make out. Strange faces turned to her—curious ones, mean ones, smiling ones, gentle ones, pitying ones. She went home thankful that soft, Swedish sounds would be there waiting and familiar loving faces would greet her.

Five

Mamma Goes to School

꿎

Two weeks went by. Pappa made record sales of his office machines.

Mamma climbed up into the attic and began to paint pictures. The smell of turpentine was like a film over everything, and Mamma had a bright look of joy about her.

Aunt Elsa found a bakery which sold the same hard candy and chocolate bonbons she bought in Sweden.

These she arranged in all the countless little dishes and pillboxes brought from home.

Sven liked his Junior High School very much and was building a model of a Viking ship for his history class.

Pelle had bumped into a boy down the street when he was out walking with Mamma. Now when his friend came to play they had day-long conversations. These talks went on in an enthusiastic language of grunts, gurgles, and gestures.

But it was Ulla who was feeling out of place.

The first few days of school she had been a curiosity. Her schoolmates thronged around her, stared at her as if she were some strange creature washed up on a beach. They tried to pronounce her name, to teach her English, and to play jacks. Oh, the attention was nice, in a queer sort of way. But jacks was a strange game, and the English words she heard made no sense. So she began sitting by herself, eating her lunches by herself, and walking home by herself.

She longed to be back in Sweden. There she had two good childhood friends at least . . . girls who had lived on the same street with her and who knew her. What were they doing now, Ulla wondered. Maybe they were tramping in the woods looking for mushrooms or having a secret meeting in the cellar of her grandmother's house as they used to do. Ulla was lonely, and she missed her old street where her friends and her grandmother lived.

It started first with just a little pinch of memory, just a small "I wish." And each day it grew until all she could think of was Grandmother. She dreamed of talking with her grandmother on the wooden settee, of singing with her by the piano, of reading with her on the scratchy horsehair sofa, of all the warm wonderful things she missed.

That's when Ulla began writing letters to her grandmother:

Dear Mormor,

I miss you awfully. I miss the things we used to do, and I miss my friends. I don't like America. I want to go back home and live with you.

Love,

Ulla

Ulla kept to herself. She stopped yelling at the top of her lungs. She stopped eating second helpings. She looked peaked and out of sorts.

Pappa was the first to notice it. He saw how frail and small she seemed going out into the blustery October weather. And her father's heart ached a bit. But from all his gardening, he knew how long it took ordinary plants to root in new ground. Wouldn't a thorny sort of plant take a longer time to set down shoots and begin to feel itself at home? Pappa kept his eye on Ulla and tried whenever he could to help her with her English. They sat together every now and again. Pappa would patiently pronounce the queer words for Ulla. But she bit her lips and stared at the letters, not wanting to say them.

Ulla grew more unhappy each day. She went out into the garden to hide in the yew tree. Many afternoons she worked herself up through the branches and found a sitting place. There she could watch the leaves let go of the surrounding trees and glide down the air. She could smell the spicy odor of evergreen. She could hear the birds massing in the gray sky. And there no one could see her. She could sit in the yew tree and cry. Now and again she felt a little better after a good cry, but it never lasted long.

Then Mamma began to notice that something was wrong. She was worried because Ulla was crying a good deal. Of course, she had cried at home in Sweden, but no more than other children. Mamma decided she must be feeling tired so she put vitamins in Ulla's milk and an extra bit of something in her lunch box. But it made no difference. Ulla was not sick. She was homesick and lonely.

Even Pelle noticed. He looked at her with great round eyes and said, "Sad Ulla."

"It's all right for you," Ulla answered. "You have a friend. But no one cares about me. Except perhaps my old friends and Grandmother." And then she wanted to cry all over again.

As time passed, Mamma became more and more concerned. Grandmother had sent her some worrisome letters about Ulla, and as a result she tried to find out from Ulla what was the matter. She asked about her school friends and about her English. But Ulla was close-lipped and strange. Mamma could learn nothing from her. She began to wonder if something was wrong at school.

One morning, Mamma decided to get to the bottom of the trouble. She was in the attic trying to paint. She squeezed the paint tubes—first vermillion and fuchsia, then azure and mauve. But none of the colors inspired her. In fact, the only persistent thing that came to mind was Ulla. And it was an Ulla with red eye rims and bristling hair, with hardened jaw and a hunched back. Mamma could have made a very modern, exciting picture out of all that, but she was much too concerned about the model itself. Mamma made up her mind to go to school and find out what was wrong. She didn't even change out of her painting clothes. Instead she put on her old brown coat, a pair of gloves to cover up the paint smudges on her hands, and, of course, the little fur piece.

She walked very fast and when she stormed into the principal's office her cheeks glowed like beacons and her eyes were the color of sea water. The principal took one look at Mamma and was instantly on guard. Mamma strode to the desk.

"What you do with my daughter, Ulla?" she asked in her awkward English.

The principal cleared his throat, shuffled his papers, and had the inspiration to ask Mamma to sit down.

"I stand, thank you," said Mamma.

Then the principal, of course, had to stand, too. It took close to an hour for Mamma to explain and for the principal to understand that there was something wrong with Ulla and that she did not seem like herself. At last, Mamma sat down and the principal sank to his chair.

It took another hour for the principal to explain and for Mamma to understand that Ulla was unhappy because she did not try to learn English and because she did not

try to make any friends. Her teacher, Mrs. Knowles, was giving Ulla special help with the language part, but it was up to Ulla to try to speak to her classmates and to make friends with them. She muttered in class, and she always chose to sit by herself. She turned away from everyone.

The principal very kindly explained that, "Ulla must project more friendliness and must overcome her reluctance to a new language and the new environment."

Mamma made him write the sentence out because it would take too long to have it explained. It was nearing noon and poor Pelle would be very hungry at home and Aunt Elsa did not know what to fix for lunch. Pappa would have to translate when he returned home. Then the mystery would be quite solved.

Mamma thanked the principal, tucked the paper in one of her pockets, and went home.

But when Pappa read the paper he said, "Humph! Such a lot of words about what we already know. Any plant needs just a bit of sun," he said, "and some good soil to get started. But it must be the right light and the right ground."

Mamma smiled. "You make it sound so simple," she said. "We shall all have to be food and light then. All of us. We must tell Sven and Aunt Elsa. Perhaps if we all help Ulla some more with her English . . ."

Pappa stroked his mustache. "English will help. But there is something more to all this. Ulla has never had to make friends before. She simply had them grow up with her. No. I'm afraid we cannot help Ulla as much as we wish. We're not the proper food or light at all."

"What shall we do then?" asked Mamma. Her heart felt empty and tired.

"We shall wait for the right light and soil to come along. It's really very simple."

But Mamma sighed and thought it wasn't as simple as all that. And Ulla went on being as bristly and unhappy as before.

Six

The Last Day of October

🙂

Now each week Ulla received postcards with silly faces on them from her grandmother. They all said much the same thing. "My little Ulla, I love you. Just see, things will go much better. I think of you very often." And sometimes in the corner one of her old friends would scribble a note to her. Ulla felt a little less lonely.

Then on the last day of October a curious stirring went through Ulla's classroom at school. It was the stirring that comes when something exciting is about to happen. Ulla could understand that stirring very well even without English because it had been the same in her classroom in Sweden. All around her, eyes glowed, elbows nudged, mouths shaped whispers and secrets. Ulla was dying to know what the excitement was all about. She could make out some of the English words, but the rest ran together in a blur and she could not understand them. There was one word that popped up between sentences. Halloween. It came again and again. Halloween . . . Halloween.

Suddenly she began to feel small soda bubbles in her stomach and the pricking of lemon on her tongue. But, by three o'clock she still had not discovered what this Halloween was. When Sven came home Ulla followed him to his room, which was next to hers.

"Can you imagine, they have witches in October instead of in the spring on Maundy Thursday," he said, throwing his books on the desk. "Have you ever heard of anything so turned around?"

"Witches, oh what? Tell me," begged Ulla.

"Everyone dresses up like a witch, or a cat, or a pirate or whatever and goes about ringing doorbells."

"Any doorbell?" asked Ulla with eyes widening.

"Any doorbell at all," said Sven. "It's the custom."

"Well, what then?" Ulla wanted to know.

They sat down on Sven's bed.

"This is what happens," said Sven. "When someone answers the door you say, 'Trick or Treat,' which means that you must receive something good to eat or you will play them a trick."

"Why, that's dreadful!" said Ulla. "It's not a bit polite."

"I told you. It's the custom. Besides, when did you ever worry about being polite?" Sven smiled at his sister. "Don't you think we should try it?"

"Yes, let's," said Ulla. And suddenly the stirring felt irresistible and she had to run to the landing on the stairs to cry, "Treek o Treet!"

At the sound, Aunt Elsa, who was sitting on her sofa, jumped three inches. Ulla had not shouted in nearly a month. And now she belted out, "Treek o Treet. Treek o Treeeeet!"

"Oh, my nerves!" cried Aunt Elsa and dropped a dozen bonbons between the cushions on the sofa.

By then Ulla was in her room. She cut a hollow rubber ball in half and put string on two sides of the rim. She placed the ball over her nose and tied the strings behind her head. Then she borrowed Sven's big black rubber boots. With Pappa's beret drawn over her stubby pig-tails she went to the kitchen to find Pelle and Mamma.

At the sight of her, Pelle burst out laughing and Mamma tweaked the rubber nose with her fingers.

"It's not the night for witches," she declared.

"In America it is," said Ulla. "And now I need to burn a cork to fix the rest of my face."

Mamma was delighted to see Ulla absorbed and ex-cited. "Things must be better for Ulla," Mamma thought. Perhaps she was growing used to school and her class-mates. Perhaps Pappa was right that they must wait for Ulla to change of her own accord. Quickly Mamma fished out a cork from one of her apron pockets. Ulla burnt the cork and drew elaborate eyebrows, black half moons above the bright blue rubber ball.

"What a sight you are!" said Mamma.

"You may paint a picture of me sometime," said Ulla generously and went to look for Sven. Pelle trailed be-hind her. Before long the three of them passed through the garden where Pappa had turned the earth and planted bulbs, making things ready for spring. They went out to the street.

Sven had dressed himself as a pirate and Pelle wore Mamma's fur piece which he had borrowed from the

clothes tree in the hall. It was a mild day. The sun broke through the trees in patches and the air seemed to smell of festivity.

"It will be a good day," thought Ulla. "I feel it. Today is the beginning of something."

At the first house they came to, Sven rang the bell. "Trick or Treat," he said, flourishing his saber and scowling behind his eye patch.

Treats were handed out all around before the door closed.

"Happy Halloween," the grown-ups said and smiled.

"Happy Halloween," the children answered and put their candy in their pockets.

They passed other trick-or-treaters and waved to them. Then they tried another door. "Let me, this time," begged Ulla.

She pressed the doorbell. "Treek o Treet," she said and smiled broadly.

It worked like magic and small lumps of candy began to bulge in their pockets. Before long there was no room left to put candy and they had eaten all they could hold. Pelle was tired and wanted to go home. Evening darkness had begun to fall.

"I don't want to stop," said Ulla. "I haven't had such

fun in a long time. I wish America was always as nice as this."

Sven saw Ulla's eyebrows raised in excitement and happiness. "All right, I'll take Pelle home and you can come when you like," he said.

"Thank you, Sven." She was quite serious now. "You are always so thoughtful and nice."

"Oh, piffle," said Sven.

"It's true. Mamma and Pappa say they can't understand how you got that way. I'm afraid I shall never be like you."

"Well then, you'll be yourself," said Sven with a grin, and he set off toward home with Pelle.

Ulla watched them go and when they turned out of sight she went up to the nearest house. It was set back from the street with thick white pine trees on either side. The trees spread out filmy branches and partly covered the windows. In each window was a pumpkin with such a happy grin that the dancing of the candles flickered out as far as the trees. Ulla went up to one of the windows and gazed at the big orange cheeks of a pumpkin. There was such shining jollity about that orange face that Ulla could not help but smile back.

"You are happy," said Ulla in Swedish. "You make

my eyes feel glad. I wish I always felt as happy as you feel."

As she stood talking to the pumpkin, the door opened and a very round little woman appeared.

"You musn't stand there so still," she said. "You'll catch your death of cold."

Ulla was startled. She turned quickly and knotted her eyebrows.

"Aye duh nut speek Eenglish," she said.

"Never mind," said the little lady and nodded her head. "You don't need English on Halloween."

Ulla understood nothing, but the word "Halloween" reminded her.

"Treek o Treet," she said proudly.

A smile broke on the little lady's face. "Treat, of course," she said and led Ulla into the hall. But first she rang the bell because she liked to hear the chimes going off from each room in the house. There was such a tinkling and echoing of chimes that Ulla's head spun to catch where the sounds were coming from.

"The bell doesn't speak English either," said the little lady. "But it speaks beautifully just the same."

Ulla wanted to push the button, too. She gazed longingly at the door. The little lady understood.

"Of course, push as much as you like," she said. "I never grow weary of that sound. In fact, I think my neighbors think I'm a bit odd. Imagine an old lady pushing her own doorbell!"

She disappeared with the ringing of the chimes and came back with a big wooden bowl of apples.

"I don't much like candy," she said. "These have all the smell and taste of autumn. We will polish yours until it winks back at you and then you shall have no better Halloween treat."

Ulla cocked her head and watched the lady rubbing shine into the apple.

"There. Take it home, dear," she said. "And come back!"

The apple fell into Ulla's hand. The little lady's hand rested ever so gently against her cheek. And Ulla felt a quiet happiness fall over her. She did not understand some of the English words but she knew very well what the hand had said.

"Happy Halloween," the little woman said.

"Happy Halloween," answered Ulla softly and turned toward the street.

Seven

Miss Merrywell

꘎

Ulla did not go back the next day. She wanted to, but she held back the way she saved the icing from a piece of cake for last. All week at school she waited for Saturday. It came at last and she let herself out by the back door and walked around the weedy part of the garden to the street.

She stood in front of the pumpkin house a good while. It had something warm about it as if the bricks themselves breathed and grew. Ulla liked it. She stood on the sidewalk gazing and relishing the friendly atmosphere.

Suddenly the door opened and the little woman came out. She had a large gardening hat on her head, a trowel in her hand, and a mattress-ticking apron tied around her full waist.

"Well now, isn't this a perfect day!" she called. "I was hoping you would come." She waved and Ulla came up the walk. "We must introduce ourselves. My name is Miss Merrywell." She pointed to her own round person.

Ulla tried to shape the words with her tongue. At last she said them.

"Mees Marrywull."

Miss Merrywell laughed. "Yes. Very good. Now, what is your name?" Miss Merrywell pointed to Ulla.

"Maye nayme is Ulla Lundgren."

"Ullah," tried Miss Merrywell, letting her tongue bounce off the roof of her mouth.

"Very guud," said Ulla and they both laughed. Then they walked together to the back of the house. Out of her pocket Miss Merrywell brought a handful of bulbs.

"It's late for these, but the ground isn't frozen yet and we can slip them in quick as anything." As she talked the gardening hat bobbed up and down pleasantly. "I'm not what they call a sensible gardener. I stick tulips in here and there. There are daffodills and crocuses stuck around, too. There must not be too much regulation. Nothing grows to regulation. I leave some space for wild things, too." Miss Merrywell pointed out swatches of weeds and thistles. "A little wildness is good for us. It is best to give it a share of space and you never can tell. Just look at my ordinary trees and shrubs that have grown up here on their own. They'll give you surprises. Little winter presents just as wild and pretty as you like. Goldenrain and ninebark. Just look at this little bladdernut and the pearl bush." Miss Merrywell strode around the garden, pointing out the bushes and trees with their pretty seed pods. "Most people are a little like one of these seed pods. After a time, they burst open and share of themselves."

Ulla did not understand Miss Merrywell, but the words fell softly and they made her feel warm. Then she watched Miss Merrywell dig a hole for each bulb and cover them with soil, just as Pappa did. Pappa liked gardening so well that he rarely let anyone help him. In fact, Ulla had only helped him once. But she was anxious to try it.

"All right," said Miss Merrywell and stood up slowly. "Would you like a turn?" She gave Ulla the trowel and a handful of bulbs and motioned toward the ground.

Ulla squatted down. It was nice to dig in the black earth. It was nice to feel Miss Merrywell's eyes on her back. It was nice to smell the autumn air. There was no need of language for those things.

After a while they went into the house. Miss Merrywell put some cocoa on the stove and placed a large platter of gingerbread on the table.

"You can't understand me," she said to Ulla, "but a hungry stomach understands food." Then Miss Merrywell laughed. "I'm afraid mine likes it too much."

They both ate and drank. Ulla let her eyes glide around the light kitchen. She noticed a yellow canary in a cage, the blue porcelain cups on the shelves, a copper teapot on the stove, saucepans on the wall in a neat row. And in a corner of the kitchen, hung close by the stove, she saw a painted tile and on it, plain as day, was written:

Kaffe tåren den bästa är
Av alla jordiska drycker

She went over to the tile and brought it down. Slowly she read the Swedish words out loud.

Miss Merrywell's eyes opened. She stood up. "Now I know how it should be said. And now I know you are a little Swedish girl. And now at last I know how we shall begin. We shall start with that very tile."

> A spot of coffee is
> The world's best drink

Miss Merrywell pointed to *Kaffe.* "Coffee," she said in English.

Ulla grinned. *"Ja,* coffee."

"Very good," said Miss Merrywell and she passed the gingerbread. "It's a good thing I learned what was written on the tile," declared Miss Merrywell, "or I shouldn't know how to go about this."

Ulla suddenly remembered Pappa's first lesson. She straightened up, stared very hard at the tile and said, "Aye weesh tou lurn."

"Yes, we have already begun," said Miss Merrywell with delight. "We shall learn much more."

Slowly they went from word to word. Ulla learned all the English words for the Swedish ones on the tile. Then Ulla began pointing at the things in Miss Merrywell's house, and she learned the English words for them. It was a game because Miss Merrywell tried very hard to learn the Swedish words for the same things. By noon they were both exhausted. Miss Merrywell brought Ulla to the living room. In the corner stood an old upright piano with a stool that wound on a spiral.

"When I'm tired," said Miss Merrywell, "I like to play the piano. It picks me right up."

Ulla touched the piano. She had not dared to look to see if there was one in Miss Merrywell's house. Now it made her tingle with familiar pleasure. There was no shiny, slick bench such as her grandmother had at home, but there *was* a piano.

Miss Merrywell sat down and played "Oh, Susannah." Ulla tapped her foot and hummed. She wanted to sing, though she didn't know the tune.

"Here," said Miss Merrywell. "Here are notes. They are so nice and international you don't need a language. If you are as tired as I am, it's good to see those round black notes and all those good familiar signs. Now, let us both sing."

That is what they did. No words came but only the nicest do-re-mi's and tra-la-la's. The music flowed into every nook and corner of the house. Soon the infection of the music was caught by the canary and he joined in. There was such a ringing and such a flowing in the music that Ulla forgot all about the time. It was nearly one o'clock when she ran home.

She burst into the kitchen where everyone was halfway through lunch. "I've found an American grandmother!" she cried in Swedish. "A real grandmother! Her name is Mees Marrywull. Mare-ee-wull," Ulla pronounced it carefully. "She lives in the house with the big pine trees outside. She has a doorbell that rings music and a piano and a bird."

"Aha," said Pappa to Mamma, "I knew we should get the right soil sooner or later. And here Ulla has found it herself."

"She's found more than that," said Aunt Elsa with a snort. "She's found her loud voice as well."

Eight

Pappa Buys a Car

Pappa walked to the train station every morning in order to catch the commuting train for New York City. The weather was growing more blustery each day and Pappa did not look forward to his morning and evening hike.

Saturday morning, in the second week of November, Pappa announced he was going to buy a car.

At the stove, Mamma stopped stirring the oatmeal. "But how can we afford a car?" she asked. "You must have left your sound business mind in New York."

"Not a bit of it," said Pappa. "I am simply tired of having to thaw out for two hours every day. I have an international license and we must have a car to go with it. We shall buy it today."

"Wonderful!" cried Sven, who liked anything mechanical.

"Dreadful," said Aunt Elsa. "We shall only be having accidents."

"Nonsense," said Pappa. "We live in America where nearly everyone needs a car, including the Lundgrens."

"I think we need some oatmeal," said Mamma and dished up their breakfast. "It will clear our minds."

"Mine is perfectly clear," said Pappa. "It is very clear that we shall have a car."

"Hurrah!" cried Sven. "May I go with you to buy it, Pappa?"

"Of course, and Ulla shall come, too. I know she's been getting some extra English lessons from her teacher and Miss Merrywell. And this will be good practice."

Ulla was not sure she wanted to go. Everyone at school still ignored her. She had been feeling lonely all week and now she wanted to spend the day with Miss Merrywell. But Pappa looked so pleased with the expedition ahead of them that she decided to go along in spite of everything.

They finished breakfast and bundled up in their heavy clothes.

"Be careful to buy a good car," said Mamma anxiously at the door.

"I think an office-machine expert, a model-builder, and a young lady with a loud voice should do very well," said Pappa, and they started off.

Each day as Pappa went to the train station, he passed a used car lot. He had already picked out the car he thought they could afford. It was a very old thing tucked away in a corner of the lot.

When the salesman heard Pappa's Swedish accent he looked very eager. Pappa let the man show him one car after the other, and listened politely as the man praised each successive car. But just as the salesman grew hopeful, Pappa shook his head. So they went from car to car. The man lost his eagerness and began to suspect that he would make no sale at all. They had heard the pros and cons of nearly every car in the lot when at last they reached the broken-down old car.

"This ain't worth anything," said the salesman. "The paint job's all gone and the engine needs tinkering. The upholstery is all popped. It's worth maybe fifty dollars. Right now it's taking up good space in my lot. But it would cost me five dollars to have it towed to a junkyard. You don't want this thing."

Pappa grinned. "Let us look," he said.

The man sighed wearily. Sven and Pappa peered under the hood. They jiggled the wires and unscrewed the caps in the battery. Then they talked. They checked the radiator and the spark plugs and talked some more. They poked at the wheels and crawled under the chassis. They decided the car was structurally sound but it was deplorably dirty, rusty, and dilapidated.

"You want it?" asked the salesman, who was getting tired and wanted a coffee break.

"What do you think, Sven?" asked Pappa.

"I think *yes*."

"I think *yes* as well," said Pappa to the salesman.

"Sixty dollars," said the man.

"You said fifty dollars before," said Pappa and looked at Ulla.

Ulla raised her voice so that it echoed across the lot to some other customers who were looking about.

"You say fifty dollars before!" she cried.

"Yeah," said the salesman and sighed.

"You said it would cost five dollars to tow away," said Pappa with a gleam in his eyes.

"Five dollars to tow away!" cried Ulla like a screech owl.

"All right, all right." The salesman raised his hands in despair. "You can have it for forty-five dollars."

"We will take it," said Pappa and showed Sven what to do to the car. Then he went with the salesman to draw up the papers.

Sven tinkered with the wires and the carburetor the way Pappa had showed him. In a few minutes, the old car splurted noisily. When Pappa came back they all three climbed in and drove home.

Pappa honked the horn in the driveway. Mamma flew down from the attic with her paintbrush still in her hand. Pelle ran to the door. Aunt Elsa hung her head out of her upstairs apartment window.

"Is that *it?*" she asked. Disapproval crackled in every word.

"Isn't it a lovely thing?" cried Sven.

"That is going too far," said Aunt Elsa.

Mamma went up to the car. She looked at it thoughtfully. At last she admitted that it had possibilities. With a quick turn of her wrist she had painted LUNDGREN

across the hood in a loud ultramarine. "Already it is better. With bright upholstery and little curtains for the side windows in the back it will look beautiful."

"With a new grease coat and a good washing it will look beautiful," said Sven.

"It will never be anything but a metal heap," said Aunt Elsa and closed her window.

Pappa smiled. "Well, Aunt Elsa had made up her mind about *one* thing at least."

Then everyone laughed and Pelle blew the car's horn. "So nice!" he squealed in Swedish.

Pappa stroked his mustache. "With Ulla's help, it came to the great expense of forty-five dollars. It is a good thing she has learned a little English."

Ulla grinned and hummed "Oh, Susannah" quietly to herself.

"It is a car with real possibilities," said Mamma, and her painting arm was already raised in anticipation.

Nine

The Long Talk

The car became the family's chief entertainment. Mamma painted it marine blue with small pea-green oak leaves like an emblem on the doors. After a few days of strong disapproval Aunt Elsa fell under its spell, too. She made organdy curtains for the side windows of the back seat. These were pulled neatly to the side and tied securely with blue ribbon. When the car was not in use, Pelle and his friend from down the street sat in the front seat and steered the motionless car to their heart's content.

Sven brought several of his friends home to work on the engine. They were the first real visitors (Pelle's friend didn't really count) to the Lundgren house. After the first time, they came nearly every day to work on the car and to eat Mamma's almond buns and jam tarts.

On weekends, when Pappa was not working in the garden, he took Mamma for rides in the car up and down the Saw Mill River Parkway. Everyone's life was brighter and livelier because of the car—everyone's but Ulla's. Of course, she thought the car was nice, too. And she greatly admired the pea-green oak leaves and the curtains. But she noticed more than ever that Sven had friends and that Pelle had a friend. Mamma and Pappa had each other and even Aunt Elsa had made friends with the baker who sold her the candy and the chocolate bonbons. And Ulla herself had Miss Merrywell, of course. But Miss Merrywell was not the same as a friend her very own age. She loved Miss Merrywell, but Miss Merrywell couldn't skip rope or play hop-scotch or do many of the other things girls like to do.

Ulla began to feel unhappy again. She started visiting the yew tree once more and her mouth wore a permanent pout as if she were constantly sucking on lemon peel.

Mamma tried to talk to her. Pappa and Sven helped her with her English as they had done all along. Even Aunt Elsa made a special effort and often invited Ulla up to the third floor. But Ulla would not be cheered. She decided everyone could have a friend except herself. And then she began to notice other people. She thought they laughed at the marine blue car and turned their noses up at the eyesore of a house in the weedy garden. At school Ulla continued to keep to herself and she thought her classmates snickered at her thick stockings and her stubby braids. She began to wonder if there was something terribly wrong with her.

Mamma and Pappa grew more and more concerned when nothing they said seemed to help. Then Mamma decided to go and see Miss Merrywell.

"All seems to go well," Mamma told Miss Merrywell over coffee one morning. "Ulla is doing better at school. Her pappa and Sven help with the teacher's special assignments. We think all is better now. Then, out of blue sky Ulla decide to be unhappy again. We stand on heads and Ulla will not notice. It is hard understanding," Mamma concluded and sighed. "Ulla comes here each day? Perhaps Ulla tells you."

"I'll try and find out what is wrong when Ulla comes,"

Miss Merrywell promised, "and I will call you."

And the very next day after school when Ulla came to visit, Miss Merrywell made her sit down by the kitchen table.

"I want to have a talk with you," she said sitting down on the other side of the table. "I want to find out what is the matter."

The kindly eyes looked gently at Ulla, who turned away from them. She stared at the wall and said nothing.

"I am your adopted grandmother, aren't I?" asked Miss Merrywell softly.

"*Ja,*" nodded Ulla and felt the hot sting of tears under her eyes.

"Well then, won't you tell me what that pout of yours is all about? Your parents are worried about you."

Ulla shook her head. Her lips trembled and one tear spilled over.

"What shall I compare you to?" asked Miss Merrywell sadly. "The things I know best are flowers and you're just like a thistle showing all your thorns at once."

Ulla cried out, "Everyone has friends! Here in America I do not have friends."

"So that is how it is," said Miss Merrywell under her breath.

"Pelle has a friend. Sven has three friends. I have no friends. At me everyone laughs."

"I don't laugh," said Miss Merrywell.

"You are a grandmother. Grandmothers do not laugh at little girls," said Ulla and blew her nose.

"Why does everyone else laugh?" asked Miss Merrywell.

"I put on funny clothes. I live in one, big eyesore house. Everyone laughs."

"Do they laugh at Sven?"

"No."

"Where does he live?"

Ulla bit her lip.

"Pelle and Sven don't have the same clothes as their friends, do they?"

Ulla shook her head.

"They also have friends who don't laugh." Miss Merrywell put her hand on Ulla's arm. "You *are* like the thistle who puts out all her thorns so that no one will hurt its downy flower. You make it very hard to be a friend. When people are pricked by the thistle they can grow angry or they can laugh. Take some thorns away, maybe they will not laugh. Perhaps they will stop to pick the flower."

Ulla thought a good while. It was true. Her feelings stuck out like barbs all over her. If she thought her classmates laughed at her, then she was sure they could never like her.

"What I feel pops out," she said at last, "and I cannot take it back."

"Maybe you don't want to take it back," said Miss Merrywell softly. "Maybe you are afraid to."

Silence fell between them. Ulla squirmed in her seat and looked at everything but Miss Merrywell. The canary shut its beady eyes against her. The saucepans marched by her on the wall. The teacups seemed to draw back in the cupboards. Only the little Swedish tile appeared to keep its place. Ulla looked at it a long while. She remembered how she had begun to learn English. Perhaps she could also learn this new thing. Slowly she raised her eyes to Miss Merrywell. Words came to her mouth, soft words that surprised her.

"Aye weesh tou lurn," she said.

"There now," said Miss Merrywell. "Three thorns disappeared right off."

Ulla smiled doubtfully. "You think so?"

"Yes. I know so."

Ten

Ulla Takes a Test

꒰ꗦ꒱

The next week Ulla tried very hard to be more friendly. From the corner of the schoolyard she tried to smile at the girls who huddled around their games of jacks. She edged over to the rope-skipping and then to the games of hop-scotch. But no one invited her to join in. No one seemed to notice her. They knew that if they did speak to her, she would only walk away. She always did. Then Ulla's lips grew stiff and her smiles would not come. A few times she tried to say "Hello" when someone was near her. But her words came in mumbles and no one heard.

At the end of one day her teacher, Mrs. Knowles, asked her to stay after school. Only then did her classmates seem to smile in a knowing, funny way. Ulla was miserable. She wondered what Mrs. Knowles could want. Finally when everyone had left, Mrs. Knowles beckoned Ulla up to her desk.

"Sit down, Ulla." Mrs. Knowles pointed to a desk in the front row. "I hope you don't mind staying a little while?"

Ulla shook her head and looked down at the desk where someone had carved a big *M* in the corner.

"I have wanted to talk with you a long time," said Mrs. Knowles slowly and carefully. "But I thought it might be too soon."

Ulla looked up and waited.

"I want to talk to you about your school work. I understand how hard it must be to learn a new language and to come to a new school. I know it hasn't been easy and you have done very well keeping up with your special assignments. But something tells me you can do even better. I know you do your homework."

Ulla nodded solemnly.

"And someone helps you when you need it?"

"*Ja*. Miss Merrywell helps," said Ulla almost in a whisper. "And Pappa and Sven." She tugged at her stubby braids and felt uncomfortable.

"It's good to have help," said Mrs. Knowles. "That's important. But in the end you are the one who must do the hard work."

"I try," said Ulla defensively.

"Yes, of course you do. But with just a little bigger try you can do ever so much better. I know you can." Mrs. Knowles smiled with a bright encouraging smile.

Ulla looked away. Everyone seemed so sure she could do things. But she, herself, was not a bit sure. At home in her Swedish school, Ulla had done pretty well. Pappa had insisted that she work hard because by the sixth grade only the children with the highest grades could go to high school instead of trade school. She worked hard in the new American school, too. But everything was different. Dividing was done all wrong and no word was spelled sensibly. In grammar there were as many exceptions as rules. Everything was confusing. It made Ulla tired even to think of it.

At home Pappa expected good work from her and

now Mrs. Knowles thought she must do better. Miss Merrywell wanted her to have no thorns. Aunt Elsa wanted her to stop shouting. Mamma wanted her to be neat. Everyone wanted something. There did not seem room for Ulla to want anything herself.

Ulla sighed. "I try more," she said gloomily.

"That's fine." Mrs. Knowles nodded with satisfaction and then she smiled secretly. "You know, there's a reason for this talk. Tomorrow we will have a spelling quiz, as you know. For a surprise, I have bought prizes for those students who make perfect scores—colored jacks if they are girls—and those high bouncing balls for the boys."

Ulla half listened and then slowly she realized what Mrs. Knowles was saying.

"I thought perhaps if you knew ahead of time," Mrs. Knowles continued, "you could study especially hard. The jacks are very pretty—and it's a nice game to ask someone else to play."

Ulla's mind raced ahead. Perhaps with jacks she could be like the others. Perhaps she could play with those girls in their little huddles. Perhaps she would meet a friend. Ulla looked up at Mrs. Knowles. Mrs. Knowles wanted her to do well. She wanted her to have friends and to be one of the girls who would win the jacks. Otherwise she would not have told Ulla about the prizes.

"Will you try very hard?" asked Mrs. Knowles.

Ulla nodded seriously.

"Good," said Mrs. Knowles and smiled. "Now it's time to go home and get ready for tomorrow."

As Ulla went to see Miss Merrywell after school she was filled with excitement. She sang "Oh, Susannah" at the top of her lungs and she thought about what Mrs. Knowles had said—"Jacks is a nice game to ask someone to play." Maybe if she won them . . . Maybe she would dare to ask someone to play with her. How often she had stood in the schoolyard wanting someone to ask her. Maybe now she could do the asking. At Miss Merrywell's she threw her books on the kitchen table with a loud thump.

"My goodness," said Miss Merrywell, watching her. "You looked pleased about something. What is it?"

"We will have a test tomorrow," said Ulla.

"Oh?"

"In spelling."

"Oh?"

"With perfect spelling I will win jacks," Ulla blurted out excitedly.

"How nice! The jacks will be a prize for a perfect score?"

"*Ja.*"

"Well now, it shouldn't be so hard to make one hundred. Here, have some sugar cookies. Then we will get to work."

Ulla nibbled as Miss Merrywell found the marked lesson in the spelling book. Then they began to drill. Miss Merrywell said one word, then another, then another. They had such queer letter combinations, not a bit like the Swedish ones. There were: OUGH's and SCH's and QUE's. Ulla's head began to ache. She felt a little discouraged. "It is very hard," she said.

"Oh, but you almost have them right," said Miss Merrywell gaily. "You do very well, Ulla. Now let's drill again."

At last they were finished. Ulla had spelled all the words correctly.

"Tomorrow you will do beautifully—just wait and see," said Miss Merrywell.

Ulla hoped she would. How she wanted to win those jacks! But the words were hard and she was not sure she could remember to spell them all.

"You will do the best you know how," said Miss Merrywell encouragingly.

Ulla nodded. "I will try," she said and smiled.

The next day in the last period of school, Mrs. Knowles told the class to get ready for the spelling quiz.

"Let's pull the desks wide apart now, and put all your books in your desks because today, for a special surprise, there will be prizes for those who make one hundred. There will be high bouncers for the boys and colored jacks for the girls."

An excited ripple went through the class. Ulla could feel her fingers growing wet around her pencil.

"We must be very careful that the prizes are won fair and square," said Mrs. Knowles. "Now, let's get ready."

Quickly the desks were straightened and the rows were made to stand wide apart so no one could see across. All the books were put away. Everyone was ready with a clean sheet of paper and a sharpened pencil. Ulla could hardly stand the waiting. All she could think of were the jacks. Suddenly Mrs. Knowles began to call out words. Ulla found herself caught off guard. She had been think-ing of the jacks. First came "though" and then "quiet" and then a string of others: "school" . . . "cough" . . . "queen" . . . "schedule."

Ulla was trying desperately to keep up. She was writing "school" when everyone else was already writing "queen." Ulla left spaces blank to keep up with Mrs. Knowles. She planned to go back to the words she had missed. But as the test continued she found herself falling behind more and more. Now she would never win the jacks. How could she catch up? She wanted the jacks very badly. If she could only look over at her classmate's paper—Nancy, the girl's name was. She was very neat. Ulla would not copy the spelling. She would only look to see which words had been called. Quickly Ulla leaned over to look at Nancy's paper on the desk next to her. "cough" . . . "queen" . . . "schedule." She wrote the words carefully on her own paper.

Now the class was writing "quaint" . . . "through." Ulla was behind again. She felt like crying. No. She had to have the jacks. She leaned over again to look at Nancy's paper. But the girl put her hand on the sheet and gave Ulla a dark stare.

Mrs. Knowles called out "dough" . . . "scale" . . . "quarter." What must Nancy think? Ulla felt shame creep around her neck like a tight rope. "Bough" . . . "scan" . . .

"quest." She was hopelessly behind. She must try to re-member the words. But she couldn't. Again she leaned over, this time to the desk on the other side of her. And there was Mrs. Knowles looking straight at her. Ulla sat back in her chair. She colored all the way to her hairline. She wanted to run—to be anywhere except where she was.

At that moment the bell for the end of school rang. The papers were collected and in great confusion Ulla rose to go. But Mrs. Knowles called to her. As the other students left they looked at her oddly, and Nancy stared at Ulla with a look that went right through her like a dart.

Mrs. Knowles turned to Ulla when everyone had left. "I never thought you would cheat, Ulla," she said sternly.

What could Ulla say? She wasn't copying the spelling, only the words. How could she explain? She had wanted the jacks so badly. In the end she didn't say anything; instead she burst out crying.

Then Mrs. Knowles did not look so cross. She sat down next to Ulla and waited, waited for the crying to stop.

"I did not want to do it," whimpered Ulla. "You go fast. I cannot remember all the words. I . . ."

"But Ulla, you know you must not cheat, especially on a quiz like this."

"*Ja.*" Ulla sobbed. "I know. I study hard. I want to win the jacks . . . but you go so fast."

Mrs. Knowles looked at her thoughtfully. "I will give you the test again," she decided.

Slowly Ulla wiped her tears and started on a new sheet of paper. Each word Mrs. Knowles gave her she wrote down. It took a long time, but when she was finished each word was correct.

Mrs. Knowles checked the paper and looked up at her. "I see you did your work, Ulla. But I cannot give you a prize. Looking over at someone else's paper is the same as cheating and cheating is not permitted. I feel very badly, but next time you must remember to raise your hand if you need help. Do you understand?"

Ulla nodded soberly. "*Ja,* I will."

"Run along home now. It's late. We will forget this."

Ulla left gladly, but to forget what happened—that she could not do. The jacks did not matter as much anymore. What mattered more was the hot sting of shame she could still feel all over her. Even if Mrs. Knowles said she would forget about the cheating, Ulla felt as if it were written on her face. She couldn't go home and face everyone—not yet—not right away.

Slowly Ulla went in the direction of home, kicking stones ahead of her and stepping over all the cracks in the sidewalk. She took her time. The afternoon light was growing dim when Ulla turned into a street where she had not been before. Once Sven had told her that the street ran into the one where they lived. But it was a longer way home and she had never tried it.

Ulla was stepping over cracks and not looking where she was going. Suddenly she became aware of someone and she looked up. There was someone on the sidewalk in front of her—a girl with roller skates on. And then Ulla recognized her. It was Nancy, the girl who sat next to her in class, Nancy who had put her hand over her paper.

Ulla did not move. Her feet felt suddenly heavy. She could not run away. Nancy was looking at her and waiting. Ulla swallowed and looked down. Again tears wanted to come. They crowded and burned under her eyelids. But she held them back.

"You cheated," said Nancy in a loud accusing voice. "I hope Mrs. Knowles punished you."

Ulla looked away. She did not want to cry. This girl

was not a teacher. She had no right to scold her. "I did not look for spelling," said Ulla stiffly. "The teacher goes too fast." Her words came out slowly, awkwardly.

"It's nasty to cheat," said Nancy and made a face.

Ulla felt as if Nancy had hit her. She had tried to explain. It was not fair.

"Cheater! Cheater!" Nancy taunted.

The words stung in Ulla's ears. She raised her hand and was about to hit the girl. Nancy drew back just in time. Then, as suddenly as she had raised it, Ulla dropped her hand and turned to go. But Nancy followed behind her on her roller skates. She was angry.

"First you cheat and then you hit!" she yelled. "Cheater! Cheater!"

Ulla's hands clenched. Her eyes burned. She turned around.

"You stop," warned Ulla. But her voice did not come out as strong as she had hoped. It was thin and wavered helplessly.

"You're a cheater," said the girl with satisfaction.

Ulla raised her hand again. She wanted desperately to hit Nancy, but somehow she didn't dare. Her hand fell and she turned on her heels and ran home.

Once in the yard she did not want to go into the house. Instead she climbed up in the yew tree and cried. Slowly the afternoon turned into darkness. The lights went on in the house, someone called for her. But Ulla kept on sitting—cold and miserable in the tree.

Eleven

Ulla Shares Her Lunch

⧏❧⧐

Mamma began to be a little worried when Ulla did not come home. It was not like her to stay at Miss Merrywell's so late. Supper was ready on the table and outside it was already quite dark. Mamma decided to call Miss Merrywell and find out what was keeping Ulla.

"Hallo, Miss Merrywell?" she said over the telephone. "Will you please tell to Ulla she must come home."

"Ulla?" answered Miss Merrywell. "She isn't here. She

hasn't been here this afternoon at all."

Mamma stared at the telephone. "Not there?" she said. "But what can have happened?" Her voice rose in alarm. "Where can she be?"

"I don't know," said Miss Merrywell. "Is there anything I can do?"

"No. No, thank you," said Mamma. "We must go to hunt now. Good-by." Mamma hung up quickly and turned to Pappa.

"She is not there. Ulla has not been there all afternoon. Oh my, what can have happened?"

"I'll go look for her," said Pappa. His face was worried as he put on his thick overcoat and went out into the yard.

"Ulla!" he cried. "Ulla!"

In the yew tree Ulla heard Pappa calling. "Ulla! Ulla!" His voice sounded raw and worried. It came through the dark, searching for her.

"Ulla, Ulla, where are you?" Pappa shouted as he walked through the back yard. Now Ulla could see his shadow coming toward her.

"Ulla! Ulla!"

Ulla stirred in the tree. Pappa stopped and listened.

"Ulla?" he said softly.

"Pappa?" Ulla's voice cracked like thin ice.

"Are you in the tree?"

"Yes, Pappa."

He came closer, standing beneath the yew tree. "What are you doing up there, ostrich? It's time for supper. Mamma is terribly worried."

Ulla did not answer. Her lip started quivering. She gripped the tree tightly and said nothing.

"Come down now," said Pappa. "It's supper time, Ulla." Pappa reached up to her.

Ulla shook her head in the dark. "I don't want . . . to eat."

"All right," said Pappa slowly. "But come down. It's very cold."

Ulla felt numb all over. When Pappa reached up she let go of the tree trunk and he caught her closely.

"What's this all about?" he asked gently.

"Oh, Pappa." Ulla buried her face in his heavy coat.

"There, there. We will talk about it."

Pappa carried Ulla into the house. The sharp lights hurt Ulla's eyes and she kept her face in Pappa's coat.

"Oh, dear," said Mamma. "Is Ulla hurt?"

"She's been run over!" cried Aunt Elsa. "I knew it would happen."

"No, no," said Pappa calmly. "It's nothing like that.

Mamma, bring a blanket to the living room and everyone else sit down and eat. We'll be along later."

Mamma scurried for a blanket and Pappa carried Ulla to the sofa in front of the fire.

"Now let's rub your hands," said Pappa after helping Ulla off with her coat. Mamma brought the blanket and wrapped her up in it. Then thoughtfully she left them.

"I think you had better tell me everything," said Pappa.

Ulla pulled the blanket around her. Slowly she began to tell about the spelling test and about the jacks and about the cheating. She told about taking the quiz again and about making one hundred. But when she got to the part about Nancy her lip began to quiver and her voice wavered.

"She called me a cheater, Pappa. She yelled and called me cheater, cheater. It was so awful." Ulla cried into the blanket.

"So?" said Pappa. "It was true, Ulla, wasn't it?"

"But I didn't mean to . . ."

"Did you ever think that Nancy wanted jacks as well? She must have worked hard, too. It wouldn't be fair for you to cheat and get jacks, now, would it?"

"No. But she will call me cheater again and I won't

ever have a friend of my own," sobbed Ulla.

"Do you remember the first lesson we had—I wish to learn?"

Ulla nodded.

"You found out wishing was not enough. You had to work to make it true, yes?"

"Yes."

"Don't you suppose that wishing for a friend is the same thing? Perhaps you must do something. Perhaps you should say you are sorry to Nancy."

"She was so mean," whimpered Ulla.

"Yes. But people are often mean when they do not understand something. Perhaps they are even a little afraid. Why don't you try to make her understand?"

Ulla thought about it. Maybe she could, but it would be hard.

"Let's have a little cold dinner," suggested Pappa, "and then you must think about it more."

"Pappa?"

"Yes, Ulla."

"I am afraid, too."

"I know. That is why it is important that you try to understand as well."

The next day was a clear, cold day. The trees along the sidewalk stood bare, and above the sky was sharply blue. Ulla felt the sting of the cold and inside her fears and worries pricked.

As she walked up to the playground before school started, she looked for Nancy. There were groups of children everywhere but Nancy was not among them. Then Ulla saw her playing hop-scotch alone on the far side of the yard. Slowly she walked over to her. Nancy looked thin and small to Ulla and yet she was afraid of her.

"Nancy," she began. Her blood beat against her temples. Her lips trembled. "Nancy," she said, "I . . . I am sorry . . . for yesterday."

Nancy stopped her game and looked at Ulla closely.

"I study hard," Ulla plunged on, not caring how her English sounded. "The teacher goes too fast in English. I cannot remember all the words. I am sorry I looked. You work hard, I know."

"Well," said Nancy. "It's bad to cheat."

"*Ja,*" said Ulla and looked down. "But English is so hard." Could Nancy understand that? Did she want to understand?

Nancy opened her mouth to say something. Then she

changed her mind and shrugged her shoulders. "I guess Swedish is pretty hard, too." she admitted.

"For you maybe," said Ulla and tried to smile a little. Then she had an idea. "May I borrow chalk?" she asked.

Nancy handed it to her. Quickly she wrote down some words.

Drottning

Tystnad

Genom

"What are those?" asked Nancy.

"Spelling words. Swedish words."

"Oh? They don't look so hard to me."

"No," said Ulla and sat down on the writing. "Spell 'Tystnad,' " she said.

Nancy stood silent. She laughed a little embarrassed laugh.

"It's pronounced so funny. The words are foreign and queer. I don't know which one you mean."

"It is the same for me in English," said Ulla and stood up.

Nancy shifted on her feet. "I guess it was pretty mean of me yesterday."

Ulla nodded.

Nancy looked at the sidewalk. "What are those foreign

words, in English I mean."

"They are same words for the test. 'drottning' is 'queen,' 'tystnad' is 'quiet,' 'genom' is 'through.' "

"Oh," said Nancy in amazement. She looked at Ulla with new eyes and was about to say something. But just then the bell for the beginning of school rang. Together they went in to begin the day.

All morning Ulla felt relieved. Nancy had not laughed at her or called her a cheater in front of the others. It had been so much easier to talk to her than Ulla had thought possible. Perhaps Nancy had understood. But if she had not, at least Ulla felt at peace with herself.

When lunch time came Ulla was content to go and sit by herself in a corner of the dining room, with braids in stray wisps, shirt tail trailing, socks falling. On the table in front of her she arranged the contents of her lunch bag: ham on limpa, an apple, a small saffron bun, two spritz cookies with almond centers and a small bag of gingersnaps. Mamma had given her some extra sweets to brighten her day. Ulla was contemplating her lunch when Nancy sat down next to her.

"Hi, Ulla," she said.

Ulla looked up, surprised at hearing her name.

"I would like to eat lunch with you, if it's all right."

Ulla looked away a moment. She couldn't believe what she had heard. Then slowly a smile grew on her face. "*Ja,* please sit," she said and waited for Nancy to arrange her lunch. Then, because she did not know what to say, Ulla raised her rich rye sandwich and bit into it.

"That looks good," said Nancy. "What is it?"

"Limpa," answered Ulla. "Mamma baked it. You can try." She handed the second half of the sandwich to Nancy. Little bulges appeared in Nancy's thin cheeks.

"It's good," she said between chews.

"*Ja,* it has fennel and anise and orange. It has good taste."

Nancy looked down. "What is that?" she asked quickly, spying the yellow saffron bun with its hidden raisins.

"Saffron bread," said Ulla and broke the bun in half. "You try."

Nancy tasted, chewing thoughtfully. "It tastes like sunshine."

"*Ja,*" Ulla nodded. Mother bakes them on holidays. We always have saffron bread on Sankta Lucia Day—the feast of light."

"What day is that?"

"It is the thirteen of December. When the saint came

to the dark north countries she brought faith and light. That is the story."

"How lovely," said Nancy. "What do you do on Sankta Lucia Day?"

Ulla enjoyed Nancy's questions. Her own answers seemed to come of themselves and she felt a pleasant excitement.

"We dress up in white. Have a party. We eat saffron bread and wait to greet Christmas. The feast of light makes us see love come."

"Oh, I wish we had something different like that before Christmas," said Nancy.

Then Ulla had an idea. Maybe Nancy would come for Sankta Lucia Day. Maybe she could ask her even after what had happened yesterday.

"Does it sound nice?" Ulla said cautiously.

"It sounds wonderful."

"You come on Sunday," she said hurriedly. "It is only three days away."

"Really?"

"*Ja.* You will have Sankta Lucia Day."

"Yes. I will. I will come." Nancy looked up suddenly. "You're a lot nicer than I thought," she said. Then she noticed that she had eaten half of Ulla's lunch. "It was so good I'm afraid I've eaten too much," she said. "You must try my lunch."

"All right," said Ulla. "I will try."

Ulla wondered at the taste of Nancy's peanut butter sandwich. The rich salty filling was nice but glued itself to the roof of her mouth.

"It is hard to eat," she mumbled trying to swallow. "It is sticking so to my mouth."

"Do you like it?" asked Nancy anxiously.

"*Ja.* I think," said Ulla.

Then Nancy produced a small package of marshmallows. Ulla gazed at the puffy white candies.

"You eat little pillows?" she asked and laughed.

"Try," urged Nancy.

The pillows were very soft to touch. Ulla pinched one between her fingers and put it in her mouth. Slowly she tasted the sweetness on her tongue as the candy melted away.

"The pillows are good," declared Ulla.

Nancy laughed. "Oh, they're just old marshmallows."

Then the bell rang for class.

"Oh dear," cried Nancy. "We have to go."

"We eat tomorrow again, yes?" asked Ulla hopefully.

"Yes, let's," said Nancy.

"Okay," said Ulla pronouncing the к as broadly as she could.

"Okay," nodded Nancy. "Tomorrow."

Twelve

Preparations

❧

Nancy nibbled on Ulla's lunch on the following day. She was introduced to *sylta* and *kaldolmar*. She tasted ambrosia cake and jelly cones. Everything in the lunch bag Ulla broke in half. Somehow the familiar tastes tasted better when there was someone trying them for the first time.

"This is such fun," said Nancy. "Let's do it every day."

Ulla grinned. *"Ja,* let us."

That evening Pappa noticed a happy glow on Ulla's cheeks and Mamma was amazed that Ulla could eat everything that went into her lunch bag. Mamma and Pappa grinned at each other. There was something new about Ulla.

"You must have help eating your lunch today," declared Mamma. "I put in enough for three today and you bring an empty bag home."

Ulla nodded. "I have help."

"Aha," said Mamma in Swedish. "I suspect something new has happened. Is your helper hungry?"

Ulla laughed. "She is very curious and very thin."

"Then we will make her fat," chuckled Mamma.

Ulla nodded and thought her mother was beautiful in her checkered apron. "Mamma, may I have that friend to come on Lucia Day?"

"*Ja*, of course, if she is to grow fat. How nice that would be for you. But I will need help to make everything on Saturday."

"We will help," promised Ulla. "I will ask Nancy."

Saturday could not come fast enough for Ulla. The morning light broke in a thin ray through the window. The sparrows were fighting over seeds in the barberry hedge and, far off, Ulla could hear the cold hiccups of a car starting.

It was Saturday. Nancy had promised to come on Lucia Day and today as well. Ulla was out of bed in a moment and into her overalls. Mamma was already in the kitchen stirring hot cocoa on the gas stove. The oven was warming up for the day's baking. The house smelled of cut pine. Sven had fetched branches from the trees at the back of the garden. Now they stood in pots on the top of cupboards and on the kitchen table. There were even pine boughs laid at the front door for the wiping of holiday feet.

On the drainboard stood four different kinds of dough in mixing bowls. The smell of yeast and sugar rose gently from them like incense. Pelle was busy licking spoons covered with cookie batter.

"But when did you make all this?" cried Ulla in amazement.

"This morning," said Mamma, "very early before the birds were up."

Slowly Pappa drifted into the kitchen for his breakfast. Upstairs Aunt Elsa smelled sweets and descended from her apartment. Soon the kitchen was filled with a sense of anticipation. Ulla looked at the wall clock. Nine o'clock. Nancy would not come just yet.

Everyone ate his breakfast quickly to make room for Mamma's baking.

"Hurry up now! Clear away! I need space," said Mamma busily.

Everyone gulped oatmeal. Aunt Elsa saw there was not yet anything besides cereal to eat and she went upstairs to tidy her apartment. Pappa disappeared to the living room with the newspaper. Sven went out and Pelle fetched some colored paper to scribble on.

Ulla watched the clock creep to nine-thirty. Now Nancy would be here in a moment. Suddenly Ulla was afraid. Would Nancy like her family? She wondered if it would be such a fine day after all? Wouldn't Nancy think they were all too odd, foreign, and different? In the midst of her thoughts, Ulla barely heard the front doorbell.

"Open! Open!" cried Mamma. "Don't keep our helper out."

Ulla ran. She pulled the front door open.

"Here I am," said Nancy. "Am I late?"

"No, no," said Ulla quickly. "Come in."

"*Ja*, come in!" called Mamma in English from the kitchen. "It's much too cold to be stamping out on the porch."

Nancy slipped in the door and looked around. The hall was full of boots and coats. Mittens lay on a heap on the linen chest in the hall. Suddenly, Pelle appeared with orange paper trailing behind him.

"Oh, you have a little brother," said Nancy and smiled at him.

"Yes. He is Pelle."

Pelle grinned and backed into Pappa who had come to the hall as well.

"Ah, I see our helper is here," he said. "But we must take her coat, Ulla."

"I am sorry. I forgot," said Ulla and helped Nancy to struggle out of her winter things.

"Now you will meet Mamma," Ulla said when everything was hung up. Together, they went to the kitchen.

"Hallo. It's a good thing you came," said Mamma and immediately covered the two girls with large aprons. "There! We can begin . . . at once."

Nancy smiled. She was a little confused by all the people but Ulla could see that Nancy did not think it was unpleasant.

Soon they had dough up to their elbows and a fine dusting of flour in their hair. They kneaded four different doughs spiced with saffron, cardamon, anise, and almond. They pushed rolling pins like steam rollers over tabletops of dough. Nancy learned how to make buns and cookies in all the traditional shapes: Christmas wagons, crescents, Turk's caps, envelopes, cockscombs, snails and vicar's hair. The girls wound the strips of dough around their fingers. The finished shapes were put on buttered pans and brushed with egg yolk. Then Mamma sprinkled the buns and cookies with sugar or raisins or nuts. Pelle ate everything that happened to spill on the table. Soon the entire room smelled of baking. It was the sweet, rich smell of bakeries and warm kitchens.

"This is wonderful!" cried Nancy. "I wish everyone had Lucia Day so they could do this."

By lunch time, the entire family hung around the kitchen door like flies around syrup.

"When ever will you be done?" complained Aunt Elsa.

"Wait, wait," said Ulla impatiently.

"When ever do we get a taste?" said Sven, mostly to tease Ulla.

"Not one more word," said Mamma sternly, "Order in the preparations is the most important thing."

"It's the only time in the year," said Pappa grudgingly. "So I suppose we must obey."

"We have guests tomorrow," reminded Mamma. "Miss Merrywell, Aunt Elsa's friend, Sven's friends, Pelle's friend, and, of course, Ulla's friend."

The way Mamma said *Ulla's friend* made Ulla's heart jump. Was Nancy really her friend? Could it be true? Ulla did not dare to believe it. She just worked harder at cleaning up.

At last, the pots were washed and put away. The buns and cookies were piled handsomely on plates. Ulla and Nancy sat down at the kitchen table, tired and happy. Mamma finally permitted the rest of the family into the kitchen. In the midst of all the baking, she had managed to cook a hearty cauliflower soup. The bowls stood steaming in front of each place at the table.

"For dessert you may have only one bun apiece," ruled Mamma. "After all, Lucia Day is not until tomorrow."

Everyone's grumpiness disappeared with that promise of tomorrow and with hot cauliflower soup in front of them.

"I suppose we don't mind waiting, then," Pappa said

and sighed exaggeratedly.

"Oh, we mind," said Sven.

"But only a little," said Nancy and winked at Ulla.

Ulla grinned. It had been the happiest morning she could remember in a long time. This afternoon she promised herself to go and tell Miss Merrywell.

Thirteen

The Feast of Light

At six-thirty in the morning on December thirteenth Sven
tiptoed into Ulla's room and shook her gently. Ulla rolled
over.

"Get up," whispered Sven. "It's time."

Ulla scampered out of bed and together they crept
down the stairs. In the kitchen Ulla put a kettle of water
to boil for coffee. Sven fetched the Lucia costumes from
the big linen trunk in the hall. For himself there was a

white robe with wide flowing arms. It was tied at the waist with a flat silver belt. In his hand he held a staff with a star on its top. On his head was a cardboard hat shaped like a cone and decorated with gold stars and half moons. For Ulla there was also a white robe and for her head she had a ring of pine boughs with six little candles.

Quickly, they fixed a tray with cookies and Lucia buns. The coffee and pine boughs were the last things to go on the tray. Cautiously, Sven lit Ulla's candles.

"Be careful," he warned.

"I will. I will," whispered Ulla excitedly in Swedish.

Slowly, they crept up the stairs again. Ulla's candles cast dancing shadows on the walls and the coffee sent a morning smell ahead of them. They made it safely to Pelle's room. From his bed he blinked at them sleepily and yawned.

"Time to get up," said Sven, and pulled him out from under the covers. "Here is your costume." It was the same as Sven's, only much smaller. Sven helped Pelle on with his things. Now they were ready.

Softly, they began singing as they walked to Mamma and Pappa's room. The light was just breaking through the windows. Ulla's candles shed a warm glow around them as they solemnly drifted up to their parent's big bed.

> *Sankta Lucia*
> *ljusklara hägring*
> *sprid i vart mörka hus*
> *glans av den fägring.*
> *Nu är luciadag*
> *Nu hörs i varje lag:*
> *Sankta Lucia!*
> *Sankta Lucia!*

"Sankta Lucia, Sankta Lucia . . ." They sang the chorus softly. They stood there, a white trio, arriving with love and a warm breakfast.

"Ahum." Pappa cleared his voice gently.

Mamma sat up in bed. "What a surprise!" she said happily.

Of course Ulla knew it was not a surprise. Just as Christmas is not a surprise each year . . . and yet it always is.

"Our first Lucia Day in America," said Pappa. "This is a fine celebration."

"Can we eat?" asked Pelle hopefully.

"But we must fetch Aunt Elsa first," cried Mamma, "or she will be left out. You go, Ulla."

Reluctantly, Ulla went. She climbed the stairs to Aunt

Elsa's apartment, singing the Lucia song off-key on purpose to get even because she wanted to stay with the others. Aunt Elsa was waiting, smiling and fidgeting at the door.

"Ulla, I'm so glad you came. I thought you would certainly forget me. Do be careful with those candles. My, but don't you look pretty. As pretty as I have ever seen you."

"Thank you," said Ulla, and she did feel pretty. Suddenly, she didn't mind having left the others to fetch Aunt Elsa. "Come down," she said. "Everything is ready."

"Yes, of course," Aunt Elsa said and bustled herself down the stairs.

They ate breakfast on Mamma's and Pappa's bed as the morning sun broke fully through the curtains.

"This is just as nice as at home in Sweden," declared Mamma contentedly.

Pappa beamed. "Of course it is."

After church everyone helped to get the Lucia party ready. Pappa lit a fire in the living room fireplace and Mamma fixed a large table of Lucia treats. Everywhere candles glowed—on the little side tables, on top of the mantlepiece, in the window sills.

"I don't know that anyone can call this an eyesore," said Mamma in Swedish when all was ready.

"It should be *eye-glad*," said Sven emphatically.

Ulla was somehow proud of it all. It was different, yes, but lovely. She hoped Nancy would think so, too. Why, even Pelle stopped to admire in the midst of his constant business.

When Miss Merrywell and the other guests came, they stopped to admire as well. Ulla watched Nancy. She was looking all around with a smile on her lips.

"Do you like it?" asked Ulla anxiously.

"Yes. It's pretty."

A quiet gaiety settled in the living room. Pelle and his friend planted themselves as close to the Lucia table as they could. Aunt Elsa on the sofa beamed peacefully at the baker and Nancy curled up on the floor by the fire with Ulla. From the rocking chair, Miss Merrywell watched everything while she talked. Sven and his friends sat on the floor discussing model airplanes and Mamma and Pappa glowed at one another as brightly as the candles.

Mamma poured coffee for the grownups and Ulla passed around the Lucia treats. Then it was time for games. They played Twenty Questions, Famous People, and Who Am I. When someone was *it* he gave hints about himself as Sven did.

"I was short. I conquered a lot of countries."

The baker guessed Napoleon, which was right. One of Sven's friends was Babe Ruth, Pelle was the man in the moon, Miss Merrywell was Queen Elizabeth, Nancy was Cinderella, Pappa was the milkman, Mamma chose to be Cezanne, a famous painter, and Ulla was Sankta Lucia herself.

"I want to know what a Sankta Lucia looks like," said Miss Merrywell. "Couldn't you show us, Ulla?"

Ulla was embarrassed.

"Please," said Nancy.

Ulla knew Sven wouldn't dress up with her when his friends were there. Perhaps Nancy would.

"Will you dress up with me, Nancy?" said Ulla softly. "You can be the star boy."

"Oh, could I?"

"*Ja.* Come, we will get ready."

The girls scurried out into the hall. Ulla helped Nancy on with Sven's costume. She had to roll the long sleeves and fold the robe up double around Nancy's little waist. When she was done Ulla surveyed her work. Nancy stood draped in the white robe with its silver belt.

"You look a beautiful star boy," she said. "Here is the hat." She put the cone shape covered with stars and half moons on Nancy's head and gave her the staff with the star on top.

"Let me look," cried Nancy. She hurried to the hall mirror to admire herself while Ulla put on her own white robe. Then Nancy helped light the candles on Ulla's headpiece and they were ready.

"Now we must sing the Lucia song," said Ulla. "It's very easy." And she hummed the song for Nancy.

"I know it!" cried Nancy. "It's an Italian tune."

"Well, then we are really ready," said Ulla, and she walked into the living room singing the Lucia song with Nancy humming at the top of her voice. When they had walked all around the room in a stately way, Nancy stopped and turned around in the middle of the room, singing proudly, "Sankta Lucia, Sankta Lucia," the only Swedish words she knew. Ulla just grinned under her wreath of candles and greens.

"How lovely!" cried Miss Merrywell.

"Why don't you sing an American song now?" suggested Pappa.

The girls whispered together and soon they broke out into "Oh, Susannah" with lusty voices. Pelle's little

friend sat and stared and Sven's friends were as polite as boys can be about dressed-up girls when there are wheels and cogs and machinery to talk about. Then the baker clapped loudly and soon everyone laughed and talked. Mamma blew Ulla's candles out and decided everyone was hungry all over again. She asked if Ulla and Nancy couldn't please pass the Lucia treats again?

They went out together to the kitchen to fetch new platters. Nancy stopped at the door.

"Ulla," she said.

"Yes?"

"Do you think your mother and father would let you come to my house?"

Ulla spun around. She could hardly believe her ears. "You want me to come?" she asked as her eyes widened.

"It would be fun to make Christmas decorations or something . . ."

"Yes, I would like," Ulla interrupted happily.

"Let's do it next Saturday. Then we would have time for some games, too. I could teach you to play jacks."

"Yes, I would like very much," cried Ulla. "I will ask Mamma now."

Soon they had fetched the new platters and together they went back to the living room. Ulla went straight to her mother and whispered something in her ear. Mamma nodded and Ulla's face broke into a grin. Then she passed the buns around.

"These are good," said the baker, taking a nibble, "professionally speaking, I mean. We shall have to have Lucia Day next year," he said and winked at Aunt Elsa. "It's much too nice not to have."

Everyone agreed to that and feasted happily until the candles burned down to little stubs. Near the fireplace Nancy and Ulla, still in their costumes, sat quietly planning for next Saturday. And as they talked the fire faded into warm coals.

Fourteen

Ulla Goes Visiting

᠌᠊᠍&

On Saturday Ulla was up early. When she came downstairs she was dressed so neatly that Mamma looked at
her in astonishment.

"Ulla!" she said. "What has happened?"

"It is Saturday, Mamma," reminded Ulla, feeling excitement out to her fingertips.

"So it is," said Mamma. "You are off visiting then?"

"*Ja,*" said Ulla and smiled.

"Well, let's fix your hair." Mamma wet a brush and brushed out Ulla's hair. Then she braided it into tight plaits.

"Let me look now," said Mamma and turned Ulla all around. "It looks nice. How long it will last I cannot promise. But then, I don't think you will worry about that."

"No," said Ulla. There was so much else to think about. Not since she left Sweden had she spent a day with a friend. Would she know what to say? Would she know what to do?

Pappa came sleepily down the stairs in his robe. "Why are you so neat?" he wondered. "Where are you off to?"

"To Nancy's house," said Ulla proudly.

"Oh yes, as if I could forget." Pappa's peppery eyes suddenly twinkled. "But aren't you a bit early?"

Ulla looked at the clock—8:30.

"No," said Pappa. "You can't go just yet, I'm afraid. If Nancy is like me she will still be sleeping."

Ulla would have to wait and when she waited she thought and when she thought she worried.

"Help me with breakfast," said Mamma as if she knew the problem exactly.

It was a noisy breakfast. Everyone talked and gave Ulla

lots of good advice about her Saturday visit.

"Don't forget *please* and *thank you,*" said Aunt Elsa.

"Don't eat all the cookies," warned Sven. "If there are any."

"Don't spill," said Pelle who had knocked his milk glass over once at breakfast already.

"Don't get in the way too much," said Mamma.

"Pooh!" Pappa exploded. "If I hear one more *don't* I'll lock all of you in the closet and go with Ulla myself."

Then everyone laughed and Ulla could feel how much they wanted her to enjoy the day.

At nine-thirty Ulla left home. Pappa waved from the porch and Pelle walked her to the end of the block. And then she was on her own. She found Nancy's street without any trouble and before she knew it she was standing in front of Nancy's house. Carefully she pressed the doorbell. Nancy opened the door.

"Hi. You made it. Come in. Mom has taken the things out to make popcorn. We can string it for the Christmas tree. We're going to decorate the tree all by ourselves. Come and look at it."

Nancy led her into the living room. The tree stood in a corner—tall and stately.

"Isn't it pretty?"

"Ja," said Ulla. "We decorate it now—so early?" she wondered.

"Sure. That way everyone enjoys it longer."

"Oh," said Ulla.

"Don't you decorate early?"

"No," said Ulla. "We wait longer. Mamma and Pappa make a surprise for us on the night before Christmas Eve. They decorate and then we see the tree the next day."

"That sounds nice, but I think it's nicer to do the decorating myself. I would hate to miss it. Come in the kitchen. We'll string the popcorn."

In the kitchen Ulla met Nancy's mother.

"Hello, Ulla. I'm so glad you could come."

"I, too," said Ulla and thought Nancy's mother was very nice.

"Here are all the things," said Nancy's mother. "Be careful."

"All right," said Nancy. "Come, Ulla. I'll show you how to make popcorn."

Ulla went to the stove. She watched Nancy pour a little oil in a large saucepan and then a handful of dry things that looked like seeds. On top of it all came the lid.

"Shake the pan over the flame," said Nancy. "Then you'll see what happens."

Ulla shook and shook. Suddenly the pan was alive. Something knocked inside and then there were lots of knocks. The lid rose by itself and steam escaped with a hiss.

"Oh!" cried Ulla. "It feels alive."

"Take the lid off," said Nancy.

Inside Ulla found the pan full of white blossoms. There weren't any seeds left.

"What happened?" asked Ulla in amazement.

"The seeds popped. They were popcorn."

"They are pretty," said Ulla.

"Taste."

Ulla tasted one but she didn't like it. "I think they are better just to make—not to eat."

Nancy's mother laughed and suggested they string the popcorn they had before making more. So the girls fetched needles and thread and strung the corn into long strands for the tree. Armed with their strands they marched into the living room. Soon the tree stood draped with garlands of corn.

"Let's see what's next," said Nancy. "Christmas balls."

Ulla watched Nancy pull out a box from the closet. It was full of shimmering balls.

"How pretty. We hang these, too?"

"Yes," said Nancy. "You're taller. Will you do the top?"

"We do not have balls for the Christmas tree," said Ulla reaching up as high as she could to hang a bright pink ball near the top.

"What do you hang then?" asked Nancy in a puzzled way.

"We hang baskets and hearts made of paper and things made of straw—goats, stars, angels. We hang cookies and candies, too. Then when the tree must come down we have a party and eat all the good things."

"You have more parties!" cried Nancy. "I hope you'll invite me."

"*Ja,* of course I will."

Then they decorated some more. When all the balls were on the tree the girls stepped back to admire their handiwork. Ulla thought it was a lovely tree. The first she had ever decorated!

"It needs icicles," said Nancy, wrinkling her nose. "It won't be right until the icicles get on there."

"What are icicles?" asked Ulla.

"Here." Nancy handed her the package. Ulla looked inside. It was filled with little silver strips.

"We hang the icicles so it looks as if the tree has snow."

Ulla watched Nancy drape the icicles on the branches. Then she took some out of the package, too. They felt cool on her hand and she liked holding them. Soon the dark green branches were covered with silver glitter and the ornaments bobbed prettily on their strings. The tree smelled fragrantly of pine and woodlands.

"It smells like a whole forest," laughed Ulla.

"Well, I'm glad we only have one tree to decorate. A whole forest would kill us," said Nancy and stood back looking critically at the tree. "There's something still missing," she said after a long while.

"What?" asked Ulla in surprise. What ever could be missing on that lovely tree?

"Wait and see," said Nancy secretly. "Close your eyes."

Ulla closed her eyes. She could hear Nancy's feet tip-toeing about. Something rustled in the room. Ulla squeezed her eyes together. What was Nancy doing? A feeling of vague excitement came over her.

"Now," said Nancy.

Ulla opened her eyes. The room looked the same. The tree looked the same. But underneath the tree was a small wrapped package.

"Open it," said Nancy and grinned.

"For me?" asked Ulla.

"Yes, open it."

Ulla leaned down and picked up the little box carefully. She undid the string. Her fingers fumbled with the paper, but then she saw what was inside.

"Jacks!" she cried. "Jacks for me?"

"Yes," laughed Nancy.

"Oh, thank you," said Ulla happily. "I wish to learn this game. I wish to learn jacks."

"Okay," said Nancy. "It's not noon yet. Come. There'll be time to learn before lunch."

Glossary

drottning	
*droh*tning	queen
Drottningholm	
*Droh*tningholm	A castle outside of Stockholm
genom	
*yay*nohm	through
Ja	
Jaah	yes
kåldolmar	
*kohl*dohllmahr	cabbage rolls
Kaffe tåren den bãsta ãr	
*Kah*feh *toh*ren dehn *beh*sta erh	A spot of coffee is
Av all jordiska drycker	
Awv *ahl*lah *yoord*iska *drŭc*ker	The world's best drink
Lundgren	
*Luhnd*grayn	
Pelle	
*Peh*leh	

Sankta Lucia

Sankta Lucia
  *Sahn*gtah Lu*s*eeah   Sankta Lucia
ljusklara hägring
  *yus*klawra *heg*ring   light clear mirage
sprid i vart mörka hus
  spreed e vahrrt *mörr*ka huhs   spread on every dark house
glans av den fägring.
  glahns awv den *faig*ring.   the luster of that beauty
Nu är luciadag
  Nu ehr lu*s*eeahdawg   Now is Lucia Day
Nu hörs i varje lag:
  Nu hörsh e *vah*rryeh lahg: Now is heard in every company:
Sankta Lucia!
  *Sahn*gtah Lu*s*eeah!   Sankta Lucia!
Sankta Lucia!
  *Sahn*gtah Lu*s*eeah!   Sankta Lucia!

ABOUT THE AUTHOR

Gunilla Norris, the daughter of a Swedish diplomat, was born in Argentina, and so her first language was Spanish. After World War II, the family moved to Sweden, and the three Dryselius children were sent to school in Stockholm, learning Swedish as their second language. When they moved to New York, English became the family's third language, but Swedish was always spoken in their home. While attending Sarah Lawrence College, Gunilla Norris met her husband David A. Norris. He is a minister at the First Presbyterian Church in Greenwich, Connecticut, where they are happily settled with their two children. *A Feast of Light* is her second book for Knopf.

This book is set in Garamond, a modern rendering of the type first cut in the sixteenth century by Claude Garamond (1510-1561). He was a pupil of Geoffrey Tory and is believed to have based his letters on the Venetian models, although he introduced a number of important differences, and it is to him that we owe the letter that we know as Old Style. He gave to his letters a certain elegance and a feeling of movement which won for their creator an immediate reputation and the patronage of the French King Francis I.

Design by Atha Tehon